Mary Anning's Curiosity

Mary Anning's Curiosity

—

MONICA KULLING

Illustrations by Melissa Castrillon

Groundwood Books
House of Anansi Press
Toronto Berkeley

Text copyright © 2017 by Monica Kulling
Published in Canada and the USA in 2017 by Groundwood Books

Groundwood Books / House of Anansi Press
groundwoodbooks.com

We acknowledge for their financial support of our publishing program
the Canada Council for the Arts, the Ontario Arts Council and
the Government of Canada.

Canada Council   Conseil des Arts
for the Arts   du Canada

ONTARIO ARTS COUNCIL
CONSEIL DES ARTS DE L'ONTARIO
an Ontario government agency
un organisme du gouvernement de l'Ontario

With the participation of the Government of Canada   Canada
Avec la participation du gouvernement du Canada

Library and Archives Canada Cataloguing in Publication
Kulling, Monica, author
Mary Anning's curiosity / Monica Kulling; illustrated by Melissa Castrillon.
Issued in print and electronic formats.
ISBN 978-1-55498-898-3 (hardcover).—ISBN 978-1-55498-899-0
(EPUB).—ISBN 978-1-55498-900-3 (kindle)
1. Anning, Mary, 1799-1847—Juvenile fiction. I. Castrillon, Melissa, illustrator
II. Title.
PS8571.U54M37 2017   jC813'.54   C2016-905756-9
C2016-905757-7

Illustrations by Melissa Castrillon
Design by Michael Solomon

Printed and bound in Canada

MIX
Paper from
responsible sources
FSC® C016245

For Susan Hughes — dear friend and
brilliant writer

The carpenter's daughter has won a name for herself, and has deserved to win it.

— Charles Dickens

Long Ago in Lyme Regis

More than two hundred years ago, a traveling fair came to the seaside town of Lyme Regis on the south coast of England. People left their tasks to go see horses jumping and riders performing stunts.

Molly Anning, expecting a child, asked her friend Elizabeth Haskings to take her fifteen-month-old baby, Mary, for the afternoon. The child was cranky with teething troubles and Molly hoped the horse show might distract and amuse her.

"She'll have a good day," assured Lizzie, cuddling Mary. "I'll make sure of that."

The pair waved goodbye and set off, crossing the bridge over the river that ran through town.

Walking on this humid August day was draining, and Lizzie stopped often to catch her breath and wipe her brow. Carrying the slight child wasn't difficult, but the heat was heavy. Lizzie saw dark storm clouds brewing overhead.

"Hope the rain doesn't ruin our day, pet," she said.

The field at the edge of town overflowed with men, women, children, horses and dogs. Lizzie spotted Lord Henry Hoste Henley, who lived at Colway Manor and owned most of the surrounding land. His hat was always the tallest and his boots the cleanest. Today he was proudly showing off his two prized shires.

Ace and Abby were draft horses able to pull felled trees or wagons weighted with full barrels. Their coal-black coats gleamed and their shaggy stockings were as white as the chalky cliffs of Dover. Lord Henley's groom had braided ribbons into their tails and manes. The pair stood patiently as people admired and petted them.

Mary wanted to pet the horses too, so Lizzie brought her closer. As the child reached out, thunder rumbled. The sound echoed around the cliffs of Lyme Bay.

Jagged lightning split the sky and a torrential rain fell. People ran for cover. Lizzie held Mary close as she raced for a tree where two women were sheltering.

"We'll wait out the storm, wee one," said Lizzie.

Suddenly, a blinding light flashed overhead. Lightning struck the tree and the three women fell down dead. Lizzie's hair was scorched and her entire right side charred. In death's grip, she rigidly clasped Mary to her chest.

Then, just as suddenly, the storm clouds blew out to sea.

People ran over to the tree to see if they could help. Dr. Fairwell was among them. He saw at once that the three women were dead and that the child was unmarked by the lightning. Could she still be alive? Was it possible?

Dr. Fairwell pried the infant from Lizzie's arms, then put his fingers to her throat. He felt a faint pulse.

Astonished, he cried, "Her heart still beats!"

Dr. Fairwell carried Mary to the Anning home down by the seawall in Cockmoile Square.

Concerned friends and neighbors followed the doctor. They were heartsick to think that Molly and Richard might lose yet another child.

Molly prepared a basin of warm water. Dr. Fairwell slowly lowered the lifeless child into the calming bath. He gently rubbed her arms and legs while Molly and Richard looked on helplessly.

Mary's eyelids fluttered, as slowly, her eyes opened.

People in Lyme Regis talked of that day for years. They called Mary Anning a "miracle child." Many were in awe of her. Others wouldn't have anything to do with her because they believed she must be the devil's own to have survived such a powerful lightning strike — one that had killed three grown women.

Certainly, Mary was never the same again. She'd been a dull and sickly baby, lacking in curiosity or spark of any kind. But, after the strike, Mary grew bright and lively. Lightning, it seemed, had startled her brain into brilliance.

PART ONE
Hard Times

1

A Birthday Surprise

May 21, 1807

During the night, a powerful storm pounded the seawall and the cliffs of Lyme Regis. A man-made breakwater, called the Cobb, created a harbor for the village and held back the highest wash of the English Channel tides. But a hard storm like this one always drenched the houses built close to the sea.

Mary Anning lived in one such soggy house. She remembered a time when the rising water had flooded the first floor and crept step by wooden step up to the second floor where the family of four slept. That time they were forced to climb out the bedroom window to escape drowning. It had seemed a grand adventure to Mary, to be perched like a gull on the rooftop, waiting for the floodwater to ebb.

East of Lyme Regis large cliffs faced the sea. The Black Ven was the cliff that rose 150 feet high above the rocky foreshore and was formed by layers of limestone, shale and soft clay. The layers were called the Blue Lias — "blue" for its shade of gray and "lias" for its layers of flat stone. The layers crumbled easily, and bashing waves regularly brought new stone treasures into view. People called these odd rock shapes "curiosities." After a hard storm, Mary's father always got up early to see if there was anything new and unusual to dig up.

Pa was a carpenter by trade. He made cabinets, boxes of every size and tables — but his first love was scouring the cliffs for fossils. Curiosities also fascinated young Mary. From the time she was five, Pa had taken her and her older brother, Joseph, along and taught them how to find curios in the cliffs and on the beach.

On this particular morning, Mary dressed quickly and made her way carefully down the dark stairwell. The oil lamps had not been lit, but Mary saw shadows and slivers of morning light peeping through the windows in the kitchen.

Suddenly, light flared out from the lamp on the dining table. Now Mary could see who had been making the shadows.

"Happy birthday, Mary!"

Pa and Joe had already gathered their collecting sacks and long poles for poking at the rocks. It was hunting time. After a storm, Pa liked to beat old Captain Cury to the best new treasures.

"I'm coming with you!" Mary said eagerly.

Pa wouldn't have minded taking her, but Mary was eight today, and that meant school — Mary's very first day.

"Time you learned to read and write," said Pa. Then he handed Mary the smaller sack he'd been hiding behind his back.

"Happy birthday, lass!"

"Open it!" encouraged Joe.

Mary plunged her hand into the sack and pulled out a hammer. Her eyes sparkled with delight when she saw what it was.

"It's a rock hammer!"

"I made it special," said Pa. "The blacksmith crafted the copper claws and the grip band. What do you think? It's got a good heft."

The hammer would make digging up new discoveries much easier.

"I'm coming with you! I'm going to dig up the giant croc with this hammer! You wait and see."

Many in Lyme Regis believed there was a giant creature — some called it a crocodile — buried in the Black Ven. Hadn't Pa been finding bits of its spine, what he called "verteberries," for years?

"Not so fast, Mary," said Ma. "There'll be no hunting this morning. Ann will be here shortly to walk with you to school."

Ma didn't like her daughter scrambling on the beach with its treacherous tides and slippery shoreline. People in the village already belittled Pa for being a fossil fanatic. Wasn't one eccentric in the family enough?

"It's grubby work for a girl," Ma muttered whenever Mary came home with hair blown wild by wind and hands creased with dried clay.

Ma wanted more for Mary. She wanted her daughter to behave in a way that wouldn't set tongues wagging and would help her make a better life than the one they were living. Ma felt she was letting her daughter down each time she allowed her to follow her father to the cliffs.

As Pa and Joe turned to leave, Joe secretly stuffed something wrapped in paper into Mary's apron pocket.

"For later," he whispered. "I'll come fetch you at school."

Father and son slipped out the door, and Mary ran to the window to watch them walking toward the beach and the dawn's early light.

When Mary heard a knock at the door, she knew it had to be Ann.

Ann Bennett lived next door. She shared the same birth year as Mary, 1799, but because she was a couple of months older she'd already started chapel school. Her father was also in the trades. John Bennett was a shoemaker.

"Happy birthday!" said Ann, handing Mary a tightly wrapped paper.

"Thank you, Ann," said Mary as she unwrapped her favorite lemon drops.

The pair started off for school with Ann telling Mary all that she might expect on her first day.

Before entering the chapel, Mary stopped to see what Joe had given her.

It was the perfect ammonite Joe had found last week. Mary had wanted to keep it, but Pa had said it was a sure sell, so she'd let it go.

"Isn't it a beauty?" marveled Mary. "Joe must have talked Pa into letting me have it."

Ann frowned. "You and your dirty old rocks."

"Aren't you at all curious about the creature that once lived inside this shell? Don't you wonder why it turned into stone or what kind of world it lived in?"

"No," replied Ann bluntly. "Never."

And that was that. Ann Bennett didn't wonder, and she rarely would.

2

Lessons at Low Tide

Joe stood outside the chapel on Coombe Street, trying to spot Mary in the crowd of girls and boys that streamed out of the white building with the arched windows.

Joe was three years older than Mary and finished with school. He hunted for fossils with Pa or helped him in his workshop, making furniture or cleaning the curiosities they found. Joe didn't want to be a carpenter like his father. Far worse was the thought of scrounging for fossils all his life. Joe wanted to learn a trade, but apprenticeships cost money. More than the Annings had.

Joe spotted Mary and shouted, "Don't hang about! Tide's out!"

Low tide came twice in twenty-four hours and gave beach hunters a few hours to explore before it swept back in, perilous and persistent. If you were caught in its sly advance you could be cut off from the footpath and dry land.

Joe was getting impatient. The beach in a gusting wind wasn't his favorite place to be, but he had an eye for finding fossils, same as Mary, and the family needed as many curiosities as they could find to sell on market days.

Mary rushed over to her brother.

"I love my ammo, Joe!" she said. "I'm making it my good-luck charm."

"Had a good first day, then?" replied Joe.

Mary nodded and smiled.

"It's nothing but an old rock, Mary," said Ann. "But it was thoughtful of Joe to give it to you."

Ann liked Joe and was always a bit shy around him.

"What's in the sack, Joe?" she asked, sweet as syrup.

Sometimes Mary thought Ann was the silliest girl she knew.

"Hunting gear, of course!" Mary replied before Joe could. "Including the rock hammer Pa made me for my birthday."

Joe turned and left, heading in the direction of the stone steps that led down to the beach.

Mary yelled, "Goodbye, Ann!" and ran to catch up.

The hard storm had brought mud, rocks and trees crashing down from the cliffs. Boulders and stones covered the sand and made walking tricky. But Mary was nimble and had been clambering on this beach for years. She knew how best to keep from slipping.

"Here's your hammer and pick," said Joe. "Be careful."

Mary didn't need a warning. The cliffs were always unstable, but after a raging storm, rock slides could happen in a blink of an eye. It would be impossible to get out of the way of a slide if you were roaming too close to the cliffs when it happened.

Further down the beach, Mary's father was hard at work. She decided to see if he had found anything. She kept her eyes on the ground as she headed in his direction. Soon she was lost in a trance, not hearing the waves behind or the gulls above, only seeing the stones at her feet.

Mary peered into rock pools full of water left behind by the tide. In one, she spotted an unusual pattern and knelt to take a closer look, her skirt trailing in the water. Under the stinking clumps of seaweed that covered the rock, Mary saw a fine line. She removed the weed and there it was, five arms, delicate as a spider's web.

"I found summat, Joe!"

Joe wasn't too far off and came over quickly.

"What is it?" he asked, kneeling beside his sister.

"It's a starfish, I think."

"Yes, it is, and a fine one too," replied Joe. "It's hard to find one with all five arms and not a single one broken off. Good job, Mary."

Pa had heard Mary and come over too. "Joe's right — it's a perfect starfish. Some call 'em brittle stars because the arms break so easily."

The fossil was embedded in a boulder that was too heavy to carry home.

"How will we bring it home, Pa?"

"We'll carve an edge around the star and bring it home in a chunk," said Pa. "But we best make haste — tide's creeping in."

Mary saw it was true. The sea was slowly slipping back. When the tide went out, it roared like a lion. When it returned, it tiptoed in like a cat on silent paws.

Pa and Joe worked together, chipping as quickly and carefully as they could. Soon they had a chunk they could carry, with the brittle star safely tucked inside.

"Never forget yourself on beach, Mary," said Pa, wrapping the rock in a rag. "A good fossil hunter is a patient one, but when the tide turns, you've got to be ahead of its rush or it will swallow you up or cut off your escape.

It's a strong wash, so always keep one eye out. Even if you could swim, you're too small to keep from being dragged out to sea."

Pa put the brittle star in his collecting sack.

"I'll carry this one," he said. "You two bring the others. Joe, take the heavier sack. It's got some fine ammonites I found at the cliff."

"Will the star fetch a good price, Pa?" asked Mary, slinging the sack with fossil tools in it onto her narrow shoulders.

"No time for talk!" yelled back Pa. "We've got to make tracks!"

"Come on, Mary!" Joe shouted, encouraging her to step lively.

They'd left it late. They were going to get their feet wet for sure.

Mary scurried to keep up with Pa and Joe who were racing for the sloping footpath beside the cliff. It led up and away from the sea and onto dry land.

The surf was surging in now. Soon it would cover the beach. The thought of being dragged far out to sea made Mary move faster.

Don't stop. Don't look back, she said to herself over and over as her shoes squelched in the wet sand.

The footpath was up ahead, but Mary could hear the breakers rolling forcefully behind her and drawing closer. Wet sand was hard to run in, and Mary's feet were chilled, but she didn't slow up.

Pa and Joe were already on the footpath. They both reached out so they could grab Mary as soon as she was close enough.

Joe shouted, "Run, Mary, run!"

It was exhilarating trying to outrace the sea. Mary fixed her eyes on the footpath and pumped her legs as hard as she could. Pa was wading in now, as far as he dared — since he could not swim either — to meet her.

Breakers rolled in swiftly. Suddenly, a huge wave pushed Mary under. Seawater filled her nose and ears as she desperately struggled to come up for air and to hold on to her sack. The tide was pulling her out to sea!

Instantly, Pa's strong arms scooped Mary up and carried her to the footpath. He didn't let her down until they were both safely on the cliff top. High tide surged in and smashed at the cliffs. Mary felt the sea spray on her face.

"I thought you weren't going to make it," said Joe, near tears.

"Let's get home quickly now," said Pa.

Before following, Mary dropped her sack and shouted, "I made it!"

And she had. In the nick of time, she'd been saved again.

3

Fossil Fish

In Lyme Regis, the houses, shops, churches, a gathering place called the Assembly Rooms, and the Cockmoile, or prison, were built on hills so steep and cobbled streets so narrow that a coach couldn't make its way into the town or to the beach. Tourists visiting from London for the bracing sea air stepped off the coach and walked or hired a small cart to carry them down.

Tourists loved to buy souvenir curios. Pa did all he could to make his fossils outshine those of the competition — namely, William Lock, better known as the Curiman or

Captain Cury. Captain Cury didn't have Pa's patience or respect for the fossils found in the cliffs. He dug them up with a spade, often damaging precious finds. He also didn't like to wait for tourists to walk down the hill into Lyme Regis. He'd meet the coach at Charmouth, five miles east of town, and sell to the passengers getting off the coach to stretch their legs.

This didn't seem right to Mary, but that was Captain Cury's way.

Saturday was market day. Pa pushed a table through his workshop window and Joe placed it on the pavement. Then he, Mary and Molly laid out all the curiosities that had been prepared that week. Pa had found a way to cut an ammonite in half using sand and water. This made the ammo's inner chambers visible. Pa's ammos shone like jewels. Tourists crowded around the Anning table to buy these special curiosities.

Pa's carpenter skills could also be seen in the wooden boxes he made to hold small curios. These were beautifully crafted with designs carved on the lid. Not only had Pa taught Mary how to hunt for fossils and how to prepare them, but he'd also taught her how to make the boxes. Ma might have hated "that grubby business," but she hated not having the rent money even more. Often, fossil sales meant the difference between beef stew for supper or plain old oatmeal.

Mary loved market days. She loved the hustle and bustle, and meeting all her neighbors. She loved the bartering and bantering. You could buy most anything — vegetables, boots and shoes, bread and biscuits, rag rugs, pottery, chairs, fresh meat and fresher fish. There was stuff to sell and stories to tell, from sunup to sundown.

Mary was gulping down her breakfast.

"Don't gobble yourself into a bellyache," warned Ma.

"I've got to help set up," mumbled Mary with her mouth full.

Ma sighed. If only Mary were this eager to help with the household chores.

Clomp-clomp-clomp!

Pa came stomping up the cellar steps, carrying a crate. Inside were the curiosities ready to sell. There were also seashells Mary had found. Pa called them bivalves.

"Kind of like ancient clams," he said. There was a batch of new ammonites that Joe had found. He was good at finding ammos. Mary was good at finding shells.

Mary brought her bowl to the sink.

"Meet you outside, Ma," she said, rushing out the door.

It was Mary's job to sort the curiosities and make an eye-catching display. She began by picking out the "devil's toenails," placing larger ones at the bottom of a rush basket, which Ma had made from the leaves of water plants, and smaller ones at the top. People thought these fossils, with their thick bony growth, looked like toenails, and not human ones! They were keen to have them because they believed they cured painful joints.

Mary lined the shells in a row. Perhaps she was best at finding shells, be they large or small, because she loved them so. She loved that sometimes shells smelled like the salty sea. She loved tracing the rough lines of the outer shell and the water-smooth insides. It set her imagination wondering about the creature that had once lived inside. What had it looked like? When did it live? And how?

People loved ammonites and could always spare a penny for even the smallest. They were thought to be good-luck charms and to ward off snakes. Once England had been overrun with snakes, so the legend went, until St. Hilda turned all the snakes into stone. Many people believed the legend and thought that ammonites were really these snakes. But Pa didn't. He was a man of science, not a believer of fanciful tales.

For example, the legend didn't explain why these fossilized snakes were never found with their heads attached. Captain Cury would often carve a head onto an ammo to fit the legend, but that was wrong according to Pa. "They're not snakes," he'd say over and over. "They're something far more mysterious."

Ma came outside, her face clouded with care. It was month's end and the rent was due.

"Do we have the rent money, Richard?" she asked, though she knew what the answer would be.

"Still short a shilling or three," Pa replied cheerfully. He never let money worry him. "Comes and goes like water, it does," he was fond of saying.

"Don't fret, Molly. The coins will come."

"But when? Surely you can't think you'll sell three shillings' worth of old stones today? I swear, some days I think we're two steps short of the workhouse."

Just then, a woman dressed in a pleated plaid skirt with a bonnet to match stopped at the table.

"What a lovely display," she said, smiling. "Do you ever find petrified fish?"

"I've never seen any, ma'am," replied Joe straight off.

The woman picked up an ammonite. "These can be found everywhere on the beach. It's the fish I am most interested in."

Mary, ever curious, asked, "Why's that, ma'am?"

Before the woman could answer, Pa said, "If it's fossil fish ye want, it's fossil fish ye'll have. Mary's a dab hand at finding seashells. I'm sure her eye can spot a fish fossil in the twitch of a cat's whisker."

"Mary should introduce herself first," chided her mother. Molly could tell this woman was educated and had money, and it didn't do to show yourself up with poor manners because you had neither.

"My name's Mary Anning," replied Mary, with a slight bend of the knee. "And this here's my brother, Joe."

"Pleased to meet you both," said the woman. "I'm Elizabeth Philpot. And to answer your question, Mary, I collect fossil fish for their rare and delicate beauty. I've made a study of them."

"I would like to see your collection one day," said Mary eagerly. "If I may," she added politely.

"Perhaps one day you shall," replied Miss Philpot. "I live up the hill in Morley Cottage with my two sisters. I'd be happy to show you my collection."

Pa spoke. "I'm Richard Anning and this is my wife, Molly. How may we help you, aside from finding the fossil fish, mind?"

"I was hoping you could build me a display case to hold my fish," said Miss Philpot. "My collection has outgrown the cases I have, and my sisters aren't happy unless my fish are under glass. They make the floors so sandy, you see."

Miss Philpot took three coins from her cloth bag. "Would this be enough for a down payment?"

"Three shillings," said Pa with a smile and a wink at Ma. "Why, yes. I do believe that's exactly right."

4

The Fall

Summer 1807

It was after supper and Pa was packing a sack with old bones. It had been a poor week for selling curios, and he had decided to walk to Charmouth to do some selling to the tourists before the coach stopped at Lyme.

"I'll be stealing a leaf from the Curiman's book," he said cheerfully. "Cut in on his sales like he does ours. Beat him at his own game."

Pa was going to meet the London-to-Exeter coach, which stopped in Charmouth, and sell to the folks outside the inn before the coach made its way to Lyme Regis.

"Is it safe to walk the cliffs this evening, Richard?" asked Ma.

A dense fog had rolled in from the gray sea and had been hanging onto the cliffs all week.

"Why not wait for a clear day?" added Ma. "After all, Charmouth isn't going anywhere."

"Can I come, Pa?" asked the always-eager Mary.

"I'll go with you, Pa," offered Joe.

"Neither of you is coming," replied Pa. "I'll be walking apace and you'll not be able to keep up. Besides, my feet know the land like the back of my hand."

Pa smiled. It was a lame joke, and no one laughed. "Wish me luck!"

With that, the tall, bearded man was out the door, bound for the cliff tops. He planned to take a shortcut across the Black Ven. This massive cliff, east of Church Cliffs, had a menacing presence even in daylight and was known for its frequent landslides.

Ma, Joe and Mary tried to keep busy that evening, each with their own worried thoughts.

Later that night, there was a loud pounding at the door. Joe was the first to make his way down the dark staircase and to open it. He saw their neighbor Mr. Bennett holding a lamp, and two other men, strangers, carrying Pa between them.

"These men found Richard at the base of the Black Ven," said Mr. Bennett.

Ma came downstairs in time to see the men lay Pa down on a mat in the kitchen by the stove.

"He was out cold, lying on the beach," one man explained.

"Lost his footing in the fog and slipped, I expect," said the other.

Ma's eyes filled with tears. She covered Pa with a blanket and hoped with all her heart that his injuries weren't serious.

"Wake up, dear one," she said, gently stroking Pa's cheek.

While Ma and Mary sat holding Pa's hands, Joe ran to fetch Dr. Fairwell. Pa's eyes were open when the doctor arrived.

"What were you thinking, walking out on the Black Ven in the fog?" Dr. Fairwell asked, opening his carryall.

The doctor examined Pa carefully, beginning with his back. At the doctor's touch, Pa winced in pain.

"You've injured your back, Richard," Dr. Fairwell finally announced. "You'll need to rest. Can you manage giving up work for a bit? I'll see what money I can get for you from the church relief fund. That way you'll rest easier."

Pa nodded, although he didn't like the idea of taking money from others.

At the door, Ma thanked Dr. Fairwell.

Then she took the large stone she'd set to warming in the oven, wrapped it in cloth and put it against Pa's back.

"How'd it happen?" she asked.

"Reckon I lost my way in the fog," replied Pa. "The ground crumbled under my feet and sent me upskittle. I rolled down with the boulders."

Pa never said another word about the accident, but, as the weeks passed, it became clear he was not himself. He was dark in his thoughts most of the time, and nothing and no one could cheer him.

Pain wracked Pa night and day, and his cries and moans upset everyone. Opium was the painkiller rich people used. The drug would have greatly eased Pa's misery, but it was expensive.

In the weeks to come, it seemed to Mary and Joe that Pa's interest in fossil hunting had died when he fell. Storms no longer excited him. He'd gaze out the window at a nor'easter blasting white foam against the house and washing the cliffs clean, and he'd remain silent. His usual excitement at such a sight was nowhere to be seen.

Pa rarely left the house now, even on days when he was able to get up and move around.

"When will you come on beach again?" Mary asked each morning.

"Not soon," was Pa's only reply.

Ma encouraged Pa to take short walks. "The sea air would do you good."

Mary thought the great crocodile might reawaken Pa's curiosity and make him want to hunt again.

"The Lyme Regis sea-dragon is out there waiting for us, Pa."

But it was no use. Richard Anning and the sea had parted ways, and that was that.

5

Hard Times

1810 — Three years later

It was still dark out, but Mary was awake and looking out the small window above her bed. The night sky looked endless, dotted with countless pinpricks of starlight. The crashing sea made Mary long to be outside.

Even though it was November and bitterly cold, Mary was sneaking out to go hunting. Before going to bed, she'd secretly packed her tools in a small rucksack and hidden it under her covers. Mary had a plan, and it spurred her on. There would be no school for her today.

Mary dressed in two skirts, two sweaters, stockings and an old wool cap of Pa's. She tiptoed down the stairs, carrying her sack and trying to make as little noise as possible.

Mary was just opening the door when she heard *"Koff-koff-koff!"*

It was Pa. Mary had forgotten. He'd been too weak to climb the stairs the night before, so he'd slept downstairs.

"Where do you think you're going?" he whispered harshly. Pa always spoke in hoarse whispers now. His constant cough had turned out to be consumption. Ma was certain the fall off Black Ven three years before had weakened Pa's lungs so that he couldn't fight off the disease when he caught it. Pa grew weaker every day.

"I'm going hunting," Mary replied gently.

Joe hadn't been soundly asleep either. He'd snuck down behind Mary and was now lighting the lamp on the kitchen table.

"You'll be late for school," he said.

"Joe's right," said Pa hoarsely. "You've got school. *Awk-awk-awk!*"

Mary saw the drops of blood in Pa's hankie and went to get a glass of water.

Pa got up from his mat and slumped into a nearby chair like a rag doll.

"I don't need to be in school to learn, Pa," said Mary, holding the glass to Pa's mouth. "Joe's learning a trade, and I'm not supposed to because I'm a girl. But I want to. Fossil hunting is my trade."

Mr. Hale, the town's upholsterer, had been kind after Pa's fall. He'd taken Joe on for a small fee that the family could afford. Joe worked hard to pay him back.

"But you *like* school," said Joe.

Mary did like school. She liked making sums come out right. She loved reading and writing. She especially loved learning new words, fancy words, words that no one in her part of town ever used. And yet Mary wanted with all her heart to do what she was best at to help her family. After all, she was eleven now.

"If anyone's going on beach to help the family, it's going to be me," said Joe.

"You've got your work with Mr. Hale," replied Mary. "You know you can't give that up. Besides, you don't love hunting the way I do."

"Enough!"

It was Ma, and she was madder than a drenched hen. She was due to have another baby soon, which would only add to the family's hardships. Lizzie had died. Percy had died. And now Ma was bringing another baby into this hardscrabble life.

Ma glared at Mary before unleashing her fury.

"Go! Give up a chance to have a better life than your pa and me. Scrounge on the beach like a tramp all your days and see where it gets you. It'll get you nowhere, of that I am certain. So go! Get out with you! School is better off without you."

Ma's words stung, but Mary didn't give them time to sink in. Instead, she shouldered her rucksack and closed the door behind her. She walked quickly down to the seashore. Hope in her heart for what she might find there took the place of Ma's harsh words.

From that day on Mary never sat in a classroom again.

Pa's final day came on the fifth of November, 1810. Mary, Joe and Ma were all beside him when he died. Pa's last words were "Stay strong."

After the funeral, when the people who'd come to cook and bring comfort were gone, Ma found out just how difficult life was going to be. Pa had left behind a large debt and there was no money to pay it.

"How will we live?" sobbed Ma.

Mary and Joe said nothing. They had no idea.

Ma's dread of the workhouse, with the shame that was attached to it, drove her to ask for church relief again. It wasn't much money, but it was enough to put some scraps of food on the table.

"Oh, Richard, how could you leave us this way?"

Joe and Mary were too sad to respond. What had Pa been thinking?

PART TWO
The Great
Crocodile

6

An Amazing Day

Spring 1811

Mary was mud splattered and bone weary, but happier than she'd been in months. She had spent the afternoon digging on the beach and was eager to tell Ma her good news. She hoped it would cheer her up. Ma had been sad since the deaths of Pa and the baby, who was born a couple of months after Pa's funeral and who had been named Richard.

Mary quickly climbed the seawall's water stairs, making sure not to slip. As she headed toward Gun Cliff, she met Ann, who fell in step with Mary's quick pace.

"Are you ever coming back to school?" asked Ann.

"No," replied Mary crisply. "Not ever. I'm too busy."

"Don't you miss it?"

Ann certainly missed Mary being in school. She missed sitting next to her in class and whispering secrets or sharing a laugh when they found something funny. Most of all, Ann missed the curious questions Mary had always asked the teacher. The class was dull without her.

The girls reached the square. Before entering her house, Mary said, "I wish you well, Ann, I do. But I've got to work."

Then Mary disappeared indoors.

Since Pa's death, Mary had kept busy — on the beach hunting or in the cellar cleaning and preparing curiosities. She went at first low tide and didn't stop until the last possible moment. Pa's debt loomed over Mary like the massive Black Ven.

Joe hunted when he could, but that wasn't often. He was busy learning how to give an old sofa a new life — by fixing the springs and adding fresh padding and fabric. Mr. Hale was also teaching Joe how to set up his own upholstery business. Until Joe knew everything there was to know, he wasn't being paid a penny, but once he had his own shop, that would change.

"I'll have a regular wage then," Joe had announced proudly.

Besides selling the fossils she found, Mary added to the family's money box by doing small odd jobs, like running errands or shopping for old Mrs. Stock who was too weak to do it herself. Mary could easily have found work cleaning houses, but she loved being outdoors. Even the coldest, most blustery days filled her with excitement and joy. Housework couldn't compare.

Ammonites sold well and, because they were plentiful on Monmouth Beach, Mary always had a good selection. Seashells sold well too. Mary felt she could find those in her sleep! One day, Mary had found a sea lily, and that had brought in enough to buy food for a day or two. She'd even found a rare fish fossil that she sold to Miss Philpot for her collection.

But the money Mary made was never enough to pay back the debt. If she could only find a fossil unlike any ever seen before, she could bring in enough money to settle the debt, with some left over besides. That desire drove her on.

When Mary came through the door, Ma was sipping tea at the kitchen table. Since the baby's death, she mostly sat and sipped tea, staring into space, with little interest in anything.

"I've something wonderful to show you, Ma!" Mary said, as she pulled out a silver coin from the folds of her hankie and plunked it on the table.

Ma took no notice of the money. All she saw were Mary's red hands.

"Your hands," she murmured. "They look like a washerwoman's, not like those of a young girl."

But Mary wasn't interested. She wanted to tell her mother about the wonderful thing that had happened on beach. Her hands could wait. Besides, Elizabeth Philpot and her sisters had concocted a cream to heal hands cracked by sand and saltwater. Mary had a small jar of it and she would use it later.

"A wonderful thing happened, Ma," Mary began. "I was packing up for home when I found a limestone clump that turned out to have a great nodule inside. I chipped at the crust and there it was, deep inside — an ammo the size of a pork pie!"

Ma smiled, lost in thought. She fingered the coin, thinking of all it could buy.

Mary continued, her excitement filling up the room that was beginning to grow dim as evening approached. "The ammo was surrounded with shale, and I knew there would be hours of work to clean it. I was wrapping it up when a fancy tourist lady came up and said she wanted to buy it. Just the way it was! Dirty with clay!

"I was so surprised to see her, dressed so fine and walking in shoes that didn't suit sand, that I didn't answer. She took my silence to mean that I didn't want to sell the ammo and offered an even higher price! She gave me half a crown for it! Can you believe it? It wasn't even clean, but she wanted it just the way it was. 'I always like to bring an unusual stone home from my walk on the beach,' she said.

"Isn't that something, Ma? The lady thought the ammo was an ordinary stone and not the long-ago creature that Pa always said it was."

Mary stood grinning. Her flood of words seemed to have cheered Ma.

"You made this much selling one ammonite?"

Mary nodded.

A half crown was enough to buy food for the week and a little besides — pork pies, bread, bacon, tea and sugar. For the first time in weeks, hope stirred in Molly Anning's breast, like a bird healing from a broken wing. But almost as quickly, hope died as the thought of Pa's debt loomed back into view.

"It's an amazing story and a goodly coin, but it'll not make a difference to the debt,

Mary," said Ma. "I fear that with each passing day, debtor's prison draws closer."

The horror of living within the confines of the prison, where people who could not pay their debts were made to live with rats, lice and other vermin, kept Ma wide-awake most nights. If they were sent there — and they would be if they couldn't soon pay the debt — would they ever get out again?

"We'll not be sent there, Ma, if we pull together," said Mary, as cheerfully as she could. "Not if I find the giant crocodile. That great beast would bring in enough to pay off the debt and blast our worries to dust!"

Ma studied Mary as though she were a stranger, then wearily shook her head.

"There's not a hope of that happening, my lass. You sound like your father when you talk like that. He always thought there was some big creature in the cliffs and spent time hunting when he should have been working at his trade. But it's like looking for a black cat in a coal cellar, Mary. Your pa gambled with our daily bread every time he spent the day on beach. He might have thought he had all the time in the world to repay his debt, but as it's turned out he didn't."

Ma sighed before she continued, "You're twelve now, Mary. It's time to face reality. You're never going to find a fossil big enough to wipe out Pa's debt. So please, let's not hear any more about it."

Suddenly, the door was flung wide and Joe burst through, shouting, "I found it, Mary! Ma! I found the great croc!"

7

The Eye in the Cliff

Joe had stumbled upon the odd shape in the cliff quite by accident. Some days after work, he went down to the beach to be close to Pa. Today, he stood studying Church Cliffs, his mind filled with memories, when suddenly he noticed an unusual shape in the limestone. It looked like a large round dinner plate. Or a monster's eye!

Was it part of a large creature? Could it be the giant crocodile Pa had talked about for as long as Joe could remember? Or was the late afternoon light playing tricks on him?

Joe stared at the saucer-sized shape. It stared back at him with a glare that made him shudder. He walked to the cliff and reached up to trace his finger around the outer edge.

"It might well be the beast," he murmured in awe.

Had he, Joseph Anning, found the fossil other hunters had never had the good fortune to find? Pa had hunted for the creature all his life, convinced that the many verteberries they'd found over the years were the vertebrae of the creature's enormous spine. Others might think these were nothing more than harmless curiosities, but Pa believed that the verteberries were bits and pieces of a larger puzzle. If you could put them together, the individual pieces would make up the spine of a creature unlike anything anyone had ever seen.

Joe thought back to the day, years ago, when Pa had brought home a large verteberry, what some folks called a dragon's tooth. It was the size of a round loaf of bread! Pa had bent over and placed the verteberry on his back.

"Can you see, by its shape, that this bone has to be part of a spine?" asked Pa excitedly.

"Now try to imagine how large the creature must have been to have a spine this big. And, it's buried in the cliffs out there, just waiting for us to find it!"

Now, as Joe stood at the cliff, another feeling took hold — that of dread. What if Captain Cury stole his great discovery? Joe would never forgive himself if that happened. But how could he keep a find this size a secret?

Joe searched the rocky beach for a suitable marker and found it in a large slab of shingle. He dragged the flat piece of rock over to the cliff and placed it at the base, below the eye.

Captain Cury was crafty.

We'll have to be crafty too, thought Joe, scuffing at the rocks and pebbles to remove his tracks from the rocky shore. Then Joe took off for home. He hoped that the Captain hadn't been watching him from the cliff top. He often did that, scoping out the scene to see who was making some great discovery that he could swipe.

Joe didn't dare look back in case it was true.

When Joe told Mary and Ma about what he'd found, Mary immediately grabbed her coat and was out the door.

"Are ye comin', Ma?" asked Joe eagerly.

"I'll see the beast soon enough," she replied, sounding lighter than she had in months. "Besides, I've got supper to get."

Joe and Mary tromped along the beach, watching where they placed their feet while keeping an eye on the cliff tops. Fortunately, Captain Cury didn't seem to be around. The sea was creeping in. There wasn't much time before high tide swept onto the beach in full force.

At the cliff, Joe scraped away the seaweed he'd used to cover up the shingle marker. He pointed to the round shape etched in the cliff's face.

"It's the monster's eye, innit?"

Seeing the curiosity again made Joe shiver. He needed Mary to say it was indeed the creature and not just his wishful thinking.

Mary stared at the eye, then merely nodded.

Finally, she spoke. "'Tis indeed the creature, Joe. Last night's storm uncovered it."

Mary tried to imagine how huge the fossil must be to have an eye this size. She stood on the slab and reached up high to touch the shape's rough surface.

"Do you think it's the whole beast, Joe?" she asked. "How will we free it?"

Joe shook his head. "I don't know. It's a powerful amount of work. I wish Pa were here. He'd know what to do."

Mary was about to suggest that Elizabeth Philpot might help when Joe tugged at her sleeve. "Don't look now, but the Captain's come into view up top, and he's seen us."

Captain Cury was short and barrel-chested. He wore an old canvas coat that came to his knees and he walked the slippery shoreline using his spade as a walking stick. The Captain had a nose for discoveries, especially those that belonged to others. You had to be clever to outwit him.

Now the wily hunter expertly picked his way down the pathway. Soon he'd reach Church Cliffs beach, and then it would be over. Their secret would be out.

Before that could happen, Mary jumped into action.

"Turn your back to the cliff, Joe, and I'll steer him away."

Mary began to meander toward the sea, keenly studying the beach as she walked. Out the corner of her eye, she saw that the Captain had taken the bait and was following her.

Suddenly, Mary dropped to her knees. She'd caught sight of something! With energy and focus, she began chipping away at the rock.

"Hey-ho! You! Anning lass!" Captain Cury's shouts boomed above the sea's pounding surf. "Found summat, have ye?"

Mary *had* found something. It was a gryphie the size of her hand — the largest she'd ever seen.

"I have," she muttered, working to free the curiosity.

The Captain peered at the Gryphaea. He'd never seen one this big either. It would sell like a hot griddle cake in Charmouth.

Joe, meanwhile, when he was sure that the Captain wasn't looking, had carefully covered the eye with wet sand and seaweed.

The Captain aimed the blunt end of his spade at the fossil.

"Let me tackle that toenail for you," he offered. "I'll dig it up right quick."

Mary jumped up and pushed the spade away.

"Not like that! The gryphie won't be worth a thing if it's in pieces."

Captain Cury gave the scrawny girl before him his fiercest look. His bullying tactics rarely failed, but Mary was far from backing down.

"Miss Mary," he said menacingly. "Your pa would be none too proud to see you give an old man grief over a common curiosity."

"It's my find," Mary replied firmly, though the comment about Pa stung. "It isn't as common as all that, and you know it."

Before Captain Cury could shove Mary aside, Joe grabbed the old man's spade. "You'll not thieve from us today, Mr. Curiman."

Mary went back to the work of freeing the gryphie. She followed the fossil's lines and left a margin. Later, she would remove the excess rock with chisel, brush and pick, and plenty of patience.

Captain Cury's next words stopped Mary cold.

"I saw the two of you mighty captivated by yonder cliffs," he said, nodding toward Church Cliffs. "I'll find what it is you've stumbled upon, though you be hiding it. I got the nose, you see." Captain Cury tapped his nose and then turned, muttering and tromping toward the cliffs that held the rare fossil.

Joe started to follow Captain Cury, but Mary pulled him back.

"Don't," she whispered urgently. "If you act to protect it, he'll twig that we're hiding summat. Then he'll not give us peace until he's stolen it."

Mary and Joe watched as Captain Cury scouted the cliff face, walking to and fro, stopping once in a while to take a closer look. They held their breaths when he stood for a long while, gazing at the very spot where the fossil lay hidden. But then he turned to leave, not seeing anything out of the ordinary, and Mary and Joe relaxed.

If the Captain found the eye and claimed the discovery as his own, Mary didn't know what she'd do. This fossil would save her family from the poorhouse, and she was bound and determined that the find should be all theirs.

Meanwhile, the young fossil hunter got busy wrapping her gryphie in a rag. "Perhaps the Curiman's eyesight isn't as sharp as yours, Joe," she said with a smile.

"Perhaps," replied Joe, but he wasn't as hopeful.

Heading home, Mary and Joe looked back only once to see if the Captain had lingered at the cliff. They were relieved to see that the incoming tide had chased him back to the footpath.

But tomorrow was another day and another chance for Captain Cury to find them out. Joe and Mary needed to be sharp to protect what was theirs. They knew it wasn't going to be easy.

8

The Fossil Shop

It was two weeks since Joe's discovery. Ma was busy with a customer when Mary and Joe burst through the door. The day after Mary brought home the half crown and Joe stumbled on the eye, Ma had the idea to turn the front sitting room into a shop.

"If ye are set on following in your father's steps, we best do it right," she'd said. "Shall we call it the Fossil Shop?"

Pa's tools were brought up from the cellar. No more standing in floodwater to clean curiosities! Display shelves and a counter were built. Mary was even able to carve a wooden sign, which now hung outside.

Since that day, Mary had worked in all types of weather, hour after hour, all the while keeping a lookout for the Captain.

Today Joe had come down to see how Mary was getting on. The weather was raw and a harsh wind had buffeted them all the way home. Now, they stood in the shop with roses in their cheeks and excitement in their eyes.

"The eye is amazing, Ma!" said Mary.

"It's only the skull, though," said Joe.

"The body of the beast is somewhere higher up," said Mary. "I'm sure of it!"

The customer, who'd had her back to the door, turned.

"What beast is this?" she asked with a smile.

Mary hadn't seen the woman standing in the corner of the room, and now she'd spilled the secret! Relief washed over her when she saw it was Miss Philpot.

"Joe found the dragon." Mary's words tumbled out excitedly. "It's buried in Church Cliffs! I've been working on the skull for days, but it's a powerful amount of work. The hardest bit will be getting the beast out of the cliff."

"We don't know how we'll do it," Joe picked up the story. "And we fear the Curiman will grab the dragon from us. He's been sniffing round. It won't be long afore he twigs."

"What dragon is this exactly?" asked Miss Philpot. She was still rather new to Lyme and, as yet, didn't know all the town's secrets.

"It's the Lyme Regis dragon, ma'am," replied Joe. "Only it's not really a dragon — probably more like a giant crocodile. Folks have been talking about it for years. I found its eye, and it's enormous."

"I'd like to help you if I may," offered Miss Philpot, catching the excitement. "It sounds like a real scientific discovery."

The keen sparkle of interest in Miss Philpot's eyes reminded Mary of Pa when he talked about how old the curiosities were, what they might be and why they were buried in the coastal cliffs. Could Miss Philpot be trusted not to take the discovery away from them?

Ma must have been wondering the same thing, for she replied, "That is a kind offer, Miss Philpot, but I'm sure we'll find a way."

Mary caught Elizabeth Philpot's look of disappointment, followed quickly by embarrassment.

"Of course, I didn't … I didn't mean …" Elizabeth sputtered.

Mary jumped in. "We'd love your help, Miss Philpot."

"We would?" asked a surprised Joe.

"Yes, we would, Joe," Mary assured him. "Miss Philpot is our friend. She'd never cheat us out of our curiosity."

"It's settled, then," said Miss Philpot, beaming. "Together we'll find a way to bring the creature to the Fossil Shop!"

It was early dawn, and the night's stars still faintly glimmered. The howling winds and lashing rain that had plagued the seaside town for days had finally ended. Mary hadn't been able to go on beach because of the storm, but today she was going to see if the waves had done their work and uncovered more of the great beast. Joe started work at Mr. Hale's first thing every morning, so he could not come along.

Mary quickly ate a bacon sandwich and grabbed her rucksack, collecting a hunk of bread for later.

The Gun Cliff houses stood black against the sea and sky. In dawn's dimness, the cliffs loomed menacingly as Mary tramped across the beach. The sea's surf rolled in beside her. The cresting and splashing of its waves were music to her ears. Overhead, hungry gulls squawked raucously.

"I'm not giving you my bread!" yelled Mary playfully.

Out of habit, Mary searched the ground as she walked, losing herself in thought. She tried to imagine the ancient sea that had once covered the land on which she walked, and all the creatures great and small — from tiny fish to ammonites to swimming great beasts —

that had teemed in it. But it was like trying to imagine how deep the sky was and how many stars it contained.

Mary had almost reached Church Cliffs when she spotted Captain Cury hobbling down the footpath. Not again! She walked past the cliffs and headed further east toward the Black Ven, where Pa had fallen all those years ago.

Mary stood before the dark, massive cliff face as Captain Cury lumbered over, using his spade to steady himself. She had seen a line in the shale and had started chipping. As she blew away rock dust, Mary saw what looked like a cluster of thunderbolts. What luck! She could keep herself busy and not let the Curiman get under her skin.

Mary worked slowly and carefully, blowing away chips and dust to reveal more of the stone shapes that lay in the rock.

"Well, well, Miss Mary," said Captain Cury, a bit out of breath. He watched Mary at work for several minutes and then said, "Is this the find you and Joe are keeping dark about?

Looks like nothing more than thunderbolts. Hardly worth the effort, it seems, being only belemnites. I find myself wondering, though, why you and your brother scurry so whenever I appear? Could it be my winning personality?"

"There's more here than meets the eye," muttered Mary, without looking up.

"So you say, but I don't believe it. There's nothing more than a thunderbolt cluster in those rocks, you and I know it. I'm off to the ledges near Charmouth where I hear there's been a landslip. I aim to find that croc, or my name's not Curiman."

With those words, Captain Cury shambled off, picking his way eastward. Mary waited until he was far down the beach before walking back to the eye. Now Mary had time to give to the work without the worry of the Captain showing up.

Mary worked tirelessly, removing the surrounding shale. She placed her hammer at shallow angles, and flakes and small chunks of stone fell away. She must not crack the bones. It would be horrible to damage this magnificent creature.

The saucer eye grew larger. Its fierce look made Mary wonder if it had died wide-eyed. She shuddered at the thought. Was it possible that a creature like this had once roamed the seas? And how long ago was that? One thousand years? Millions of years?

Elizabeth Philpot had told Mary that some of the world's geologists believed the earth had gone through many different ages and was millions and millions of years old. That certainly wasn't what church folk were taught.

"It boggles the brain," Mary had said with a mixture of fear and wonder when Elizabeth Philpot told her.

The knowledge gave Mary even greater admiration for the creature that had once swum freely and was now being uncovered by a fossil hunter's hammer.

9

Who Owns Those Bones?

Tap-tap-tap!

Mary worked hard, harder than she ever had before. The giant eye was now joined by a long snout and a tangle of jagged teeth. The thought of how shocked folks would be when she, "poor Mary Anning of Bridge Street," sold the skull and saved her family from ruin, drove Mary on.

"Hello!" came a shout from above. It was Elizabeth Philpot.

Miss Philpot rarely came on beach. Now the woman from Morley Cottage was walking slowly and carefully, step by step, down the footpath in her fine shoes. Then she crossed the sand and timidly picked her way over the stones. Though she didn't do it often, the middle-aged woman didn't lose her balance. Mary was impressed.

Miss Philpot stood away from the cliff and silently gazed at the creature. She drew closer and removed a glove so that she could run her hand along the long, pointed snout and the jagged teeth.

"The skull is *massive*," she said, her voice filled with awe. "The expression in its eye looks horrified at being buried alive. Might it have died in a sudden cataclysmic event, I wonder?"

Mary had no answer to that. Instead, she responded, "I think the rest is buried higher up. I feel it in my bones."

Miss Philpot smiled, but Mary wasn't joking.

"I found many verteberries that must belong to its spine. The beast would be worth plenty more if I could find it all. Maybe the next big blow will uncover it."

"Perhaps," agreed Miss Philpot, not wanting Mary's hopes to get too high. "For now, though, we have our work cut out for us and, I think, the Day brothers are just the pair to help. I've hired them to lift the creature from its grave."

Mary smiled, grateful. She'd lain awake nights wondering how she would ever remove the giant skull and bring it to the shop.

Two brothers named Davy and Billy Day came to do the work. They were stonecutters, and they had the tools needed to cut blocks of concrete, and strong backs to carry the weight.

"Is it real?" murmured Davy nervously when he saw the skull.

"Might it be a stone carving?" suggested Billy.

"It's a fossil," replied Miss Philpot. "Once it was a living creature. Now it is frozen in time."

"How can that be?" asked Davy, mystified.

But before Miss Philpot could answer, Mary interrupted.

"Can you pull it from the rock and bring it to the shop?" She was eager to get on with it.

"Aye, to be sure!"

"Aye, in a wink!"

Davy and Billy got to work, forgetting the nature of the beast they were freeing from the cliff. They stuck wooden wedges into the gaps in the layers of shale. They pried and pulled the creature out in three chunks: first the snout, then the eye and finally, the side of the head that was embedded in the rock. They laid the pieces on a canvas stretcher with poles at either end.

"Off we go!" said Miss Philpot cheerily. For if truth be told, she had doubted the job was possible.

The brothers were strong, but all the same, they grunted and groaned as they labored up the narrow footpath's incline.

"Careful. Careful," they kept repeating the word to each other.

In Cockmoile Square, it was rent day, and Lord Henley was making the rounds. When he spotted the brothers carrying the heavy load, he came over to take a look.

"What have ye here?" he asked, touching the creature's teeth.

Lord Henley looked long at Mary before he spoke. "I heard tell you'd found something in my cliffs and wondered when I might find out about it. You do know this creature belongs to me, don't you?"

Mary was about to speak, but Lord Henley raised a gloved hand.

"No. Don't say a word. I own the land where it rested, so it naturally follows that the beast is mine. However, I am not an unfair man and will pay you for it."

Mary frowned. She didn't want to sell the skull without the body.

Before Mary could answer, Elizabeth Philpot came to her defense.

"Mary would gladly sell you the fossil, Lord Henley, but not merely the skull. She believes the body remains hidden in the cliff and that a good storm will reveal it. Once Mary has found and prepared it, you will be adding a creature to your collection the like of which no one has ever seen. For a fair price, of course."

Lord Henley scowled at the woman from London. However, his icy stare did not succeed in getting her to back down. Miss Philpot stood her ground.

"The body may never be found even if it exists, and I'm not sure that it does," said the squire. "And I mean to have this creature for my collection. Why don't I buy the skull now and the body whenever — if ever — it is found?"

"If Mary believes the body belonging to this skull lies somewhere in the cliff, I believe her. Why not let her do things her way? In the end, the curiosity will be yours, however things unfold."

"All right, then, I'll give you one year," replied Lord Henley gruffly. "If the rest of the curio doesn't surface by then, I'll be adding the skull to my collection."

"For a fair price," added Miss Philpot.

"For a fair price," replied Lord Henley, defeated. Then he turned on his heel and left.

Mary and Miss Philpot exchanged a triumphant look.

In the Fossil Shop, the Day brothers heaved the massive weight of the eye onto Mary's long worktable. After putting the other pieces on the floor, they left. The creature's leering grin filled the room.

"It's a gruesome thing," murmured Ma. "What do you make of it, Miss Philpot?"

"Our lives are built on mystery, Molly. We know so little about how the world around us came to be that I dare not hazard a guess."

Miss Philpot had little trouble believing that a beast such as this one had once swum in an ancient sea. Science was endlessly fascinating to her, and each and every day, new things were coming to light.

"It's a mystery monster!" Mary said. "We'll be rich when I find the body!"

Just then, Joe walked in. His day at Hale's was over. When he saw the pieces of the curio, he gave a whistle through his chipped front tooth.

"We can pay off Pa's debt with the money from this one!"

"I have an idea," said Miss Philpot. "Once Mary's finished the cleaning, and you've encased the skull in a protective frame, Joe, let's put it on display. I think people would be willing to pay a penny to see something this rare. It would be like going to the London museum. And you could make a little money sooner rather than later."

Over the next few weeks, Mary busied herself with picks and brushes, cleaning the limestone that encased the skull. She carefully chipped and brushed away debris, bringing into focus the clean lines of the skull with its fierce grandeur.

When Mary was done, Joe built a frame around it, and the Days proudly carried the curiosity over to the Assembly Rooms where it was put on display.

Miss Philpot had been right. People wanted to see the giant crocodile, and every day more and more found the penny to take a peek. It was like seeing a two-headed cow or a cat with no face. It was a freak of nature.

Even Captain Cury came for a look. When he'd had an eyeful, he said to Mary, who was standing nearby, "I wager you'll be seeking the body now, Miss Mary. Well, don't let your hopes fly up too high. I'll be looking for that part of the beastie, myself."

With that, the Curiman left the building, banging his gorse-bush walking stick on the varnished oak floors.

10

The Great and Terrible Lizard

For months Mary watched and waited. If wild storms came when you wished for them, the coastline would have been pummeled hundreds of times over — for Mary made that wish each day. But the storms that smashed the coast that winter didn't uncover the body that was buried deep in the cliff.

Mary went fossil hunting every day and returned with the usual curiosities, but not a shred of good news. Perhaps she'd been wrong about the creature's body. Perhaps it was only the skull that was to be her great discovery.

Ma tried to be encouraging. "It will happen," she said, "if it's meant to be."

Then came a winter storm that lasted for days and had everyone worried for their safety. Gigantic waves bashed and battered the cliffs, drenching the houses that stood near them. Many quaked in their homes, sure they'd be washed out to sea, but not Mary. Her spirits rose as her hope was renewed. She could hardly wait for the blow to end!

At the first calm dawn, Mary excitedly tramped down to Church Cliffs. The sea glimmered in the morning light and gulls shrieked their greetings. Mary breathed in the tangy sea air. It was wonderful to know where she belonged.

Mary tromped steadfastly eastward. When she reached the spot where the skull had been, she slowly scanned the limestone ledges and the bands of shale of the Blue Lias. She sought out places where crumbling layers had been washed away by smashing waves to reveal what was underneath. Mary was searching for the slightest hint of the creature's spine.

As Mary scoured the cliff, she thought of the book Miss Philpot had shown her.

A French natural scientist named Georges Cuvier had written it. Cuvier studied living animals and compared their skeletons to those of fossilized creatures, and the book was filled with his drawings. Mary immediately noticed that Cuvier's drawing of a crocodile skull didn't match the skull she'd uncovered. The snout wasn't right. The eye was too large. So what kind of creature was buried in the cliff?

Suddenly, Mary saw a ridge of humps in the limestone. Were these the beginnings of the creature's spine? Mary scraped at the mud and shale, uncovering a long line of bumps that could only belong to a spine. She'd been right! When it died, the sea creature's head and body *had* separated. The body was a little higher up from where Mary had excavated the skull.

The monster fossil lay waiting to be freed from the cliffs. And what a monster it was!

"Ahoy there, young Mary!" shouted a familiar voice. "What have ye found?"

Oh, no, thought Mary. *How could I let him creep up on me?*

Captain Cury was banging down the beach, balancing on slippery rocks with the expert use of his spade. When he finally reached Mary and saw what she'd been staring at, he gave a long, low whistle.

"So, ye've beat me to the beast."

"I have," Mary replied. "Just so you know, it's mine."

"I knew ye'd be the one to find it, for ye be the miracle girl. Innit right?"

"What do ye know 'bout that?" Mary asked quickly. She didn't like being reminded of the day three women were struck dead and she was spared. It sent shivers through her.

The curiosity man gave Mary a rare smile. His teeth were all but gone. The ones that remained were brown with rot. All the same, the smile made him look years younger.

"I was present on the day that bolt struck you and the three ladies nestled under the elm. The lightning strike felled the women, but not you, a wee babe. Oh, no, not you. You were being spared for this day. I knew ye'd make a name for yourself."

Mary was uneasy. Why should this man, who'd stolen many a fine fossil from her since Pa had died, be speaking like a friend? Mary was happy she had the beast, it was true, but her achievement felt hollow without Pa there to share her happiness. He couldn't show pride in Mary's hard work, which he would have done if he'd been alive. And now, to top it off, Captain Cury was being nice to her! The world had turned on its head.

"You think my kindness be a trick, young Mary?" asked the Captain, his eyes warm and watery. "Well, there's only the one trick. I'm old now and don't wish to die with an enemy standing at my grave."

Mary accepted the Captain's words, and together they stood awestruck by the outline in the cliff.

Finally, the Captain spoke. "What is this great beast, I wonder?"

"It's a sea reptile, for certain," said Mary thoughtfully. "A giant swimming creature, but not a crocodile."

"And you're certain of this because …"

"Because of the French scientist's book Miss Philpot showed me."

"I see," replied the Captain. "Mayhap he be right."

When the rest of Lyme Regis found out what Mary had discovered, you'd have thought the King of England was coming to visit, there was that much excitement. The Day brothers built a stronger, higher platform so Mary could stand at the height of the bones to do her work. Joe helped when he could. Ma and Miss Philpot were excited too, and often brought Mary hot tea and crumpets to encourage the young fossil hunter.

People who hadn't been to the beach in years came down to see young Mary Anning at work. Even Ann, impressed, came to see what her friend had discovered.

"It's a frightful thing," she murmured. "You're amazing to have found it."

But Mary was chip-chip-chipping away and didn't hear her friend's words. After that day, Ann never came back to the beach, for the creature frightened her.

The daily work of hammering at shale and rock to bring the creature closer to the light rested on Mary's shoulders, and she accepted the responsibility without complaint. Each day she came down to the shore with a light heart, knowing she was going to uncover more of the creature. She imagined it might be like working on a sculpture, watching rock take on a new shape under her hand. What would her chisel uncover today? What would the creature look like when she finished?

On cold, blowy days, Mary secured herself to the platform with Pa's belt. She wore gloves with the tips of the fingers cut off, so she could feel the fossil buried in the stone and not damage any of the fragile bones.

Because Mary had found the creature within a year from the time she found the skull, Lord Henley let her finish the job of freeing the great and terrible lizard from its grave. Mary worked for months. Her hands grew rough and red, but Ma didn't say a word. She just rubbed Miss Philpot's cream on them each night.

Finally, the day came when the creature's entire body was revealed. The beast was ready to be removed.

Once more, the Day brothers cut large blocks in which the fossil was embedded. They brought the pieces to the Fossil Shop. When the bones were clean, Mary varnished them. While she had been carving the creature out of the cliff, Mary had kept the curiosity damp with wet sand. Now, indoors, the varnish Pa had used for his wood pieces would stop air from drying it out.

The limestone slabs were cemented into another frame built by Joe, and Mary added a skim of lime plaster to set the bones and make the finish appear smooth. The beast was ready.

Mary stood back to admire her work. The large creature had paddles instead of legs, and its tail had an odd little kink in it. It was thirty feet long from the tip of its snout to the end of its tail. It lay across the workshop, through the hall and partway into the kitchen.

Molly was looking forward to having the creature gone.

"Your pa would be so proud of you, Mary," she said, on the day Lord Henley was to pick it up. "To think, a mere lass, with little schooling, did what those great scientists do all the time — and all of them big men, mind. It boggles my mind, it does. I can't help but wonder what else you are destined to do."

"I agree with your mother," added Miss Philpot, who'd come over to see the fossil off. "You have what it takes to find many more such wonderful creatures."

The squire pulled up his rack-bed wagon, which was used for hauling heavy loads.

"Ace and Abby are the only horses strong enough to pull this weight," he said once the Day brothers and Joe had managed to wrangle the beast on board.

"Here's your money, Molly, minus the rent you owe me," said Lord Henley, giving Molly a wad of large banknotes. "You did fine work, Mary. Keep me in mind should you find another beastie."

With a tip of his hat, the squire was gone, and with him Mary's curiosity.

Through the many months of hard work, Mary had come to call the creature her own, and now it was gone. Her heart felt empty and sad at its loss.

"There are no other beasties to be found," she murmured sadly.

"You can't know that for certain, Mary," said Miss Philpot. "There may be many, many more. We live in a world filled with mystery."

Mary smiled. Of *that* she was certain.

Author's Note

More about Mary Anning

Mary Anning was born with a natural scientific curiosity and an uncanny talent for finding fossils. As a child, she followed her father onto the seashore and quickly learned from him how to find, collect and excavate curiosities, which was another word used to describe fossils. As Mary grew, so did her passion for collecting fossils. It became her life's work.

Mary Anning made many major discoveries. She was the first person to collect, display and correctly identify ichthyosaurs, plesiosaurs and pterosaurs. Mary's fossil finds forced geologists (the word "paleontology" wasn't in use until 1822) to revise their theories about the Earth's age. Years after Mary was gone, Charles Darwin proposed his own theories in his book *On the Origin of Species,* which was published in 1859. He used Mary's fossilized creatures as evidence that living beings change or evolve over millions of years.

Mary's first major discovery was the ichthyosaur, whose unearthing is described in this story. The creature was dolphin-like in shape and ranged in size from 15 to 30 feet (4.5 to 9 m). Ichthyosaurs had big eyes, sharp teeth, four fins and fish-like tails. They breathed in air with lungs and gave birth in water to live young. We know this about them from the fossilized bones of baby ichthyosaurs that have been found inside the bones of adults.

In 1823, Mary uncovered the first complete *Plesiosaurus* ("near lizard"). This reptile was nine feet long, with a broad body and a short tail. It was also a marine reptile. It used its four pointed flippers, shaped like paddles, to swim in the ancient sea. Plesiosaurs were among the first fossil vertebrates to be described by science. And Mary Anning was responsible for finding them.

In 1828, Mary found a nearly complete specimen of a pterosaur, or "winged lizard," which lived 66 to 228 million years ago. The pterosaur was a flying reptile related to the dinosaur. Pterosaurs were the first animals, after insects, to fly using wing power. They evolved into dozens of species — from those as small as paper planes to those as large as fighter jets. When Mary made the discovery, the headlines at the time announced that she had found the bones of a "flying dragon."

One of Mary's most intriguing puzzles concerned the fossilized clumps she frequently found. Collectors called them "bezoar stones." They were found in the abdominal region of ichthyosaur skeletons. Mary's curiosity once again sparked her desire to find out what these fossil clumps could be. She broke one open. Inside, there were fossilized fish bones and scales, as well as the bones of smaller ichthyosaurs. Mary's astute observations led the geologist William Buckland to conclude that bezoar stones were, in fact, fossilized feces. Buckland named them "coprolites," meaning dung stones.

Buckland also suspected that the spiral markings on the fossils proved that ichthyosaurs had spiral ridges in their intestines that were similar to those of modern sharks. It was Mary Anning's discoveries and observations that helped geologists like William Buckland come to a better understanding of many prehistoric creatures.

By the time Mary died at age forty-seven from breast cancer, she was known in geological circles in Europe and America. However, because she was a woman, Mary was never allowed to join the Geological Society of London. Nor was she always given full credit for her scientific contributions.

Even so, Mary Anning's discoveries have contributed to our knowledge and understanding of prehistoric life. In 2010, the Royal Society of London named Mary Anning one of ten British women who have most influenced the history of science. Not bad for someone with so little schooling!

What Is a Fossil?

Fossils are the skeletons of animals, plants, fungi and single-celled living things that have been preserved over millions of years. There are two types of fossils — body fossils and trace fossils. A body fossil is the fossilized body of a once-living creature. A trace fossil is the impression a creature has left in the sediment by its activities — for example, footprints, tracks, fossilized eggshells, nests or burrows.

In this book, Mary and the other fossil hunters uncover many kinds of body fossils. Ammonites were free-swimming mollusks living around the same time that the dinosaurs walked the Earth and disappearing during the same extinction event. They ranged in size from tiny species measuring less than an inch (2 cm) across to large ones reaching over 6 feet (2 m) in diameter. They had big heads, large eyes and tentacles.

They were animals without backbones similar to our modern-day squid, cuttlefish and octopus.

People thought the coil-shaped shelled creatures were coiled snakes turned to rock. That is why they were often called "snakestones," when they weren't being called "ammos." The name "ammonite" comes from the ancient Greeks. They believed the shells looked like the horns of a ram, so they named them after the Egyptian god Amun or Amon, because he was often shown wearing ram's horns.

Belemnites, like ammonites, belong to the group known as cephalopods. They were called "bellies," "ladies' fingers" or "thunderbolts" because people once believed that these fossils came from the heavens during thunderstorms. Belemnites were similar to the modern squid in the way they moved through water. Also, when under threat, they would squirt a cloud of ink in the water.

Verteberries or crocodile teeth were believed to come from crocodiles, but were actually the six-sided vertebrae of an ichthyosaur, as Mary would learn once she'd uncovered her great croc.

Devil's toenails or gryphies were a fossil bivalve related to the living oyster, scientifically called Gryphaea.

Brittle stars were spiny-skinned creatures like starfish and sea urchins. The crinoids, cousins to brittle stars, look like beautiful plants when fossilized. They were called "sea lilies."

What Happened to Mary's Monster?

Lord Henry Hoste Henley paid the Annings 23 pounds sterling for the fossil that everyone thought was a giant crocodile. That doesn't sound like much, but in the 1800s it was more money than the Annings had ever seen at one time. It made a dent in Richard Anning's debt, as well as put food on the table.

But Lord Henley wasn't honest. He didn't add Mary's fossil to his collection. Once he owned it, he turned around and sold the croc for a profit to William Bullock's Museum of Natural Curiosities in London. William Bullock dressed the fossil in a vest and placed a monocle over its eye. A sign pinned to the vest read "Crocodile in a Fossil State." Mary's magnificent creature was nothing more than a freak in a freak show. And no one thought more of it than that.

On a visit to London to visit her brother, Elizabeth Philpot saw Mary's "crocodile." She was shocked and saddened to see the colossal creature that had once prowled an ancient sea made to look so ordinary and foolish. Mary was hurt and angry when Elizabeth told her about it. All her months of hard work hardly seemed worth it.

Then, in 1817, the fossil was sold once more, but this time to the British Museum (Natural History). Off came the vest! The monocle was thrown into the trash. Mary's sea monster was given a proper scientific name — *Ichthyosaurus*, which in Greek means "fish lizard."

Ichthyosaurs evolved from being "fish lizards" with fins into a streamlined fish-like form and remained at the top of the food chain until they were replaced by plesiosaurs. The identification of this predatory marine reptile opened up a new way of thinking about the age of the Earth, about evolution and extinction.

The Seashell Song
She sells seashells on the seashore.
The shells she sells are seashells, I'm sure.
For if she sells seashells on the seashore,
Then I'm sure she sells seashore shells.

We all know this little rhyme, but did you know that many think Mary Anning may have been the inspiration for it? In 1908 Terry Sullivan wrote the words and Harry Gifford the music for this song that was sung onstage in what was then called pantomime. Terry Sullivan most likely visited the seaside town and heard the story of the girl who found fossils in cliffs and seashells just by walking on the beach.

The Jurassic Coast Today

Today the cliffs and shore where the Anning family hunted for fossils is a World Heritage site. The layers of sedimentary rock in the cliffs along the Jurassic Coast are, as they say, "a walk through time." They reveal the Earth's evolution across 185 million years and form a near-complete record of the Triassic, Jurassic and Cretaceous periods. The 95-mile stretch of coast — between Exmouth in East Devon and Studland Bay in Dorset — is a favorite among tourists, as it was in Mary's day. It attracts those who love the hunt or who simply wish to learn more about the famous fossil finder.

The Lyme Regis Museum

The Lyme Regis Museum stands on the spot where Mary Anning's childhood home once stood. In 2011, Mary Anning's famous ichthyosaur returned to Lyme Regis on the 200th anniversary of its discovery. Folks got a chance to see Mary's curiosity up close in the setting in which it was found. A few months later, the fossil was returned to the Natural History Museum in London, where it is still displayed.

Mary Anning's Fossil Shop

Most of the events in this story happened as I have described them, although I have taken a liberty with the timeline. Mary was twenty-seven years old when she set up a shop in the house she bought for her mother and herself. For the sake of my story, however, I opened the shop some years earlier.

Molly Anning's Children

I chose not to include Mary's younger siblings in this story, partly because not one of them lived to adulthood and partly because I wanted to focus on the relationship Mary had with her older brother, Joseph, who was instrumental in finding the eye of the skull. Richard and Molly Anning had as many as ten children, but most died of disease. Their first-born, also named Mary, died at age four when her clothes caught fire. Mary was named for her. Joseph and Mary lived to become adults, which was something of a miracle in those days.

For Further Reading

These books made researching Mary Anning and her world interesting and fun.

Curiosity by Joan Thomas. McClelland & Stewart Ltd., 2010.

The Dinosaur Hunters: A True Story of Scientific Rivalry and the Discovery of the Prehistoric World by Deborah Cadbury. Original publication Fourth Estate, 2000. HarperCollins Publishers, 2010.

The Fossil Hunter: Dinosaurs, Evolution, and the Woman Whose Discoveries Changed the World by Shelley Emling. St. Martin's Press, 2009.

Jurassic Mary: Mary Anning and the Primeval Monsters by Patricia Pierce. Original publication 2006. The History Press, 2015.

Remarkable Creatures by Tracy Chevalier. Dutton, 2010.

Selected Books for Young Readers

Finding Wonders: Three Girls Who Changed Science by Jeannine Atkins. Atheneum Books for Young Readers, 2016.

Mary Anning: Fossil Hunter by Sally M. Walker, illustrated by Phyllis V. Saroff. Carolrhoda Books, Inc., 2001.

Rare Treasure: Mary Anning and Her Remarkable Discoveries by Don Brown. Original publication 1999. Houghton Mifflin Harcourt Books for Young Readers, 2003.

Stone Girl, Bone Girl: The Story of Mary Anning by Laurence Anholt, illustrated by Sheila Moxley. Original publication Orchard Books, 1999. Frances Lincoln Children's Books, 2006.

Acknowledgments

Thank you, Sheila Barry, for your encouragement and editorial wisdom. They mean the world to me. Thanks also to the terrific Groundwood team — Michael, Nan and Emma — for their expertise; and to the amazing Melissa Castrillon who created the magical cover and interior art. And, as always, thank you, Nancy!

This project received a Writers' Reserve grant from the Ontario Arts Council, for which I am grateful.

MONICA KULLING is the author of more than fifty books for children. Her most recent book is *On Our Way to Oyster Bay: Mother Jones and Her March for Children's Rights*, illustrated by Felicita Sala. She has also written the popular Great Idea series, including *Spic-and-Span! Lillian Gilbreth's Wonder Kitchen*, which won the Flicker Tale Award given by the North Dakota Library Association. Monica's books have been nominated for many other awards, including the Norma Fleck Award for Canadian Children's Non-Fiction. Among her recent picture books are *Happy Birthday, Alice Babette; Grant and Tillie Go Walking* and *The Tweedles Go Electric*. Monica lives in Toronto.